Kidnapped!

Introduction — Volume 3: The Loss of the Brig

In June 1751, upon his parents' death, 16-year-old David Balfour left the small Scotland town of Essendean to travel to "the house of Shaws," the estate of his only living relative, Ebenezer Balfour. The uncle proved a greedy old man, living in a huge, decaying old house, and even tried to trick David into falling to his doom from a great height. David came to believe that his late father Alexander was the older brother and should have inherited the estate.

Ebenezer lured David to the Queensferry docks on the promise he could speak with a lawyer named Rankeillor, who knew the Balfour family's history. But Ebenezer had secretly arranged for David to be kidnapped by a Captain Hoseason of the Covenant, and destined for a life of servitude in the Carolina colonies. Only the second mate, Mr. Riach, treated David with any kindness.

Days out of port, the ship struck a small boat, whose only survivor was Alan Breck Stewart. Alan was an exiled Scottish Jacobite—one who desired to see James of Scotland on the British throne. James' supporters had been brutally defeated half a decade earlier. Alan offered the Captain money to take him to Linnhe Loch in Scotland, but Hoseason schemed instead to overpower him and seize his beltful of gold. David warned Alan, and together they fought off the ship's crew, taking control of the ship's main cabin, or roundhouse. Alan exulted in his own fighting prowess, but when the two of them stood triumphant, David sobbed at the realization that he had shot men in battle…

Writer: Roy Thomas

Penciler: Mario Gully

Inker: Jason Martin

Colorist: Sotocolor's

A. Crossley

Letterer: David Sharpe

Cover Artist: Gerald Parel

Production: Taylor Esposito

Special Thanks –

Allo, Suter, Nausedas, Ginter, Sankovitch

Assistant Editor: Nathan Cosby

Editor: Ralph Macchio

Editor in Chief: Joe Quesada

Publisher: Dan Buckley

Spotlight

MARVEL®

VISIT US AT
www.abdopublishing.com

Reinforced library bound edition published in 2011 by Spotlight, a division of the ABDO Group, 8000 West 78th Street, Edina, Minnesota 55439. Spotlight produces high-quality reinforced library bound editions for schools and libraries. Published by agreement with Marvel Characters, Inc.

Printed in the United States of America, Melrose Park, Illinois.
042010
092010
This book contains at least 10% recycled material.

Library of Congress Cataloging-in-Publication Data

Thomas, Roy, 1940-
  Kidnapped! / adapted from the novel by Robert Louis Stevenson ; adapted by: Roy Thomas ; illustrated by: Mario Gully. -- Reinforced library bound ed.
      p. cm.
  "Marvel."
  Summary: Retells, in comic book format, Robert Louis Stevenson's tale of sixteen-year-old David Balfour who, after being kidnapped by his villainous uncle, escapes and becomes involved in the struggle of the Scottish highlanders against English rule.
  ISBN 978-1-59961-781-7 (vol. 1) -- ISBN 978-1-59961-782-4 (vol. 2) -- ISBN 978-1-59961-783-1 (vol. 3) -- ISBN 978-1-59961-784-8 (vol. 4) -- ISBN 978-1-59961-785-5 (vol. 5)
  1. Scotland--History--18th century--Juvenile fiction. 2. Graphic novels. [1. Graphic novels. 2. Scotland--History--18th century--Fiction. 3. Adventure and adventurers--Fiction.] I. Gully, Mario. II. Stevenson, Robert Louis, 1850-1894. Kidnapped. III. Title.
  PZ7.7.T518Kid 2010
  741.5'973--dc22
                                    2009052844

All Spotlight books have reinforced library bindings and
are manufactured in the United States of America.

As soon as the day began to break, I climbed a hill...

...the ruggedest scramble I ever undertook.

When I got to the top, I saw no sign of the brig, which I supposed had lifted from the reef and sunk.

Nor, in what I could see of the land, was there either house or man.

Weary and hungry, I set off eastward along the south coast...

...hoping that, by the time the sun had dried my clothes, I might find a house...

...and perhaps get news of those I had lost.

NEXT: *DEATH IN THE FOREST*